PENDRAGON

The Guide to the Territories of Halla

D. J. MacHale
Illustrated by Peter Ferguson

Aladdin Paperbacks
New York London Toronto Sydney

For my awesome nephews Taylor and Chris

—D.J.M.

This book is a work of fiction. Any references to historical events, real people, or real locales are used fictitiously. Other names, characters, places, and incidents are the product of the author's imagination, and any resemblance to actual events or locales or persons, living or dead, is entirely coincidental.

ALADDIN PAPERBACKS
An imprint of Simon & Schuster Children's Publishing Division
1230 Avenue of the Americas, New York, NY 10020

Designed by Debra Sfetsios
Manufactured in the United States of America
First Aladdin Paperbacks edition May 2005
2 4 6 8 10 9 7 5 3 1
Library of Congress Control Number 2004108341
ISBN 1-4169-0014-4

Table of Contents

HALLA

EVERYTHING THERE EVER WAS, ALL that will be. This is Halla. Ten territories that coexist across time and space, each with its own unique culture and character. From the tropical jungle that is Eelong, to the ocean-covered world of Cloral, to the rugged mountains of Denduron, each has its own distinct personality. But as different as they may be, the territories of Halla have one thing in common.

They are doomed.

A demon who ironically calls himself Saint Dane has made it his goal to crush the territories, throwing them into chaos so that he alone can control all there ever was, or will be. Saint Dane commands no army. He does not invade with weapons and soldiers. His strategy is far more devious. He presents himself as a friend who wants nothing more than to help foster prosperity. But in truth, he guides the trusting people of the territories into making decisions that will lead them to ruin. He is tricking the people of Halla into destroying themselves. No one sees him coming. No one knows his plan. He has the power and the will to single-handedly bring about the downfall of all that exists. The only hope of stopping him rests with a small band of brave people who have dedicated their lives to saving Halla: **the Travelers.**

Each territory has but one. All were raised not knowing their true destiny until the day they were given a mission. They were shown the wondrous flumes that would whisk them between territories. They were warned that each territory is unique, and that people and objects from one cannot be brought to another. They were given the greatest challenge of all time: to protect their home territories from Saint Dane. And they were given a leader—a young boy who had to leave his family, his friends, and his comfortable life in order to guide this courageous group of Travelers in their quest.

Bobby Pendragon.

This special illustrated volume gives us a chance to experience the wonders of Halla as only Bobby has. We have learned of his adventures through his journals. He has described in great detail the danger, the excitement, and the fear of traveling through time and space to hunt down Saint Dane. Now for the first time we will see some of these amazing sights for ourselves.

We are going to get a peek at Cloral, Denduron, Veelox, Eelong, and the Earth territories. We will meet the Travelers: Loor, Vo Spader, Aja Killian, Alder, Gunny VanDyke, and Kasha. We will also see some of the colorful characters Bobby has run across on his adventures, like Maximillian Rose from First Earth and Dr. Zetlin from Veelox. And we will get a glimpse of the man who first introduced Bobby to his true destiny: Uncle Press.

Oh yes, Saint Dane is here, too.

This book is your private flume into the territories. As you travel through the pages, discovering old friends and learning secrets you never imagined, keep one thing in mind: **This is only the beginning.**

THE CHARACTERS

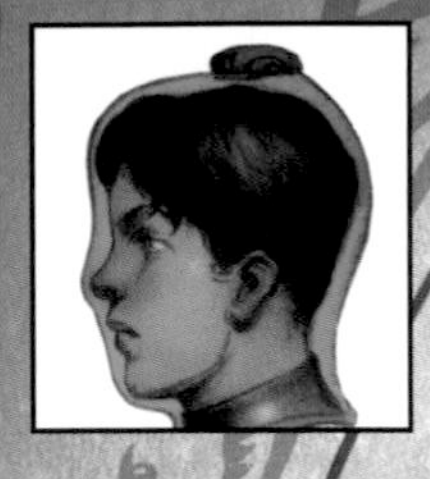

BOBBY PENDRAGON
The lead Traveler from Second Earth

SAINT DANE
The Demon Traveler

PRESS TILTON
The original Traveler from Second Earth

AJA KILLIAN
The Traveler from Veelox

VO SPADER
The Traveler from Cloral

Loor
The Traveler from Zadaa

Max Rose
The mob boss from First Earth

Nancy "Jinx" Olsen
The daring pilot from First Earth

Vincent "Gunny" VanDyke
The Traveler from First Earth

Alder
The Traveler from Denduron

Kasha
The Traveler from Eelong

THE MERCHANT OF DEATH
The quig spotted us. Or maybe it had smelled us. It didn't matter which because either way, it was starting to circle for the attack.
—Bobby Pendragon, Journal #3

The Adventure Begins.

Bobby Pendragon is about as normal a fourteen-year-old as can be. That is, until the night his uncle Press takes him from his quiet little home in Connecticut to the abandoned New York City subway station where Bobby first sees the flume—an incredible portal that rockets them across time and space to a distant territory called Denduron.

There Bobby finds himself in the middle of a brewing civil war between peasant farmers and the elite ruling class that forces them to slave in gem mines deep underground. Saint Dane takes the role of advisor to the gluttonous queen, fueling her greed, pushing her to demand even more from the poor peasants, which only fires their desire for freedom, and revenge.

Together with Uncle Press; Loor, the warrior Traveler from Zadaa; and Alder, a knight and Traveler from Denduron; Bobby reluctantly takes on the challenge of preventing a war that could tear the territory apart. They must battle prehistoric bears, legions of knights loyal to the queen, peasants who treat them as traitors, and an unlikely foe who unknowingly holds the key that could either save—or destroy—Denduron.

Saint Dane

He is a dangerous, deadly chameleon who can transform himself into anyone he desires in order to blend into a territory.

Loor

Traveler.
A warrior-in-training from the territory of Zadaa. She is a skilled, fearless fighter and Bobby's closest ally.

Message Pages

Bobby's precious journals. He documents all that is happening to him as a Traveler, and sends them to his best friends, Mark Dimond and Courtney Chetwynde, for safekeeping on Second Earth.

Skull of Figgis

A victim of the Tak mines—
and Saint Dane.

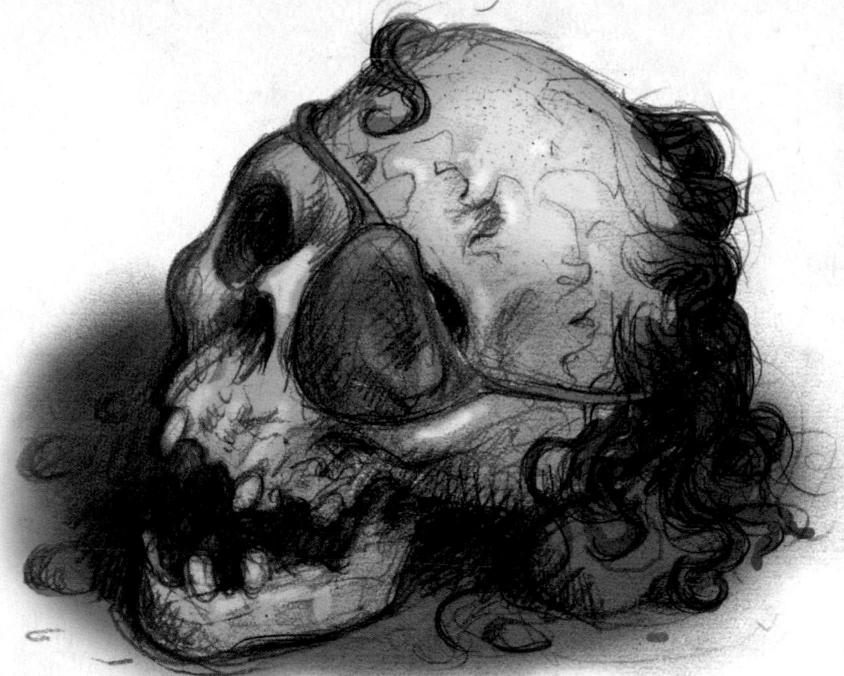

glaze

The most precious item on Denduron.
This stunning blue mineral comes at a high
price, for the mines are choked with
poisonous fumes that are deadly
to the miners.

Tak Bomb

The Milago miners of Denduron
plan on using this load of the
explosive mineral to destroy the
glorious castle of their vicious
taskmasters, the Bedoowan.

DENDURON

Territory Era: 124—The Year of Rising Light

Principal Tribes: Bedoowan, Gallauao, Milago, Novan, Revenian, Toom

Population: Approximately 12,300,000

Three suns: Noab, Laa, Rigg

Landmass: Fifteen continents: three inhabited (Bedoo, Nodd, and Galla), 12 uncharted

Oceans: Nine. The largest, Tinitebian, surrounds the continent of Bedoo where the Bedoowan and Milago tribes live.

Highest peak: The Mountain of Orloo (on the continent of Nodd). At 29,112 feet, it is taller than Mount Everest of Second Earth and three times as tall as the mountains of Loom near the Milago village.

Climate: Inhabited continents along the meridian are temperate. Uncharted continents to the north and south are frozen.

Currency: Quills. (One quill = approximately three U.S. dollars)

Time measured in: Marrs (One marr = approximately one hour)

Major holidays: Feast of Noab (Milago holiday to celebrate the harvest), Kukura (Novan holiday that rejoices in the creation of the stars), Runnow Taa (Bedoowan holiday of music)

The Traveler: Alder

Alder

Traveler. The gentle yet skilled fighter who must battle his own people to save his home territory from Saint Dane.

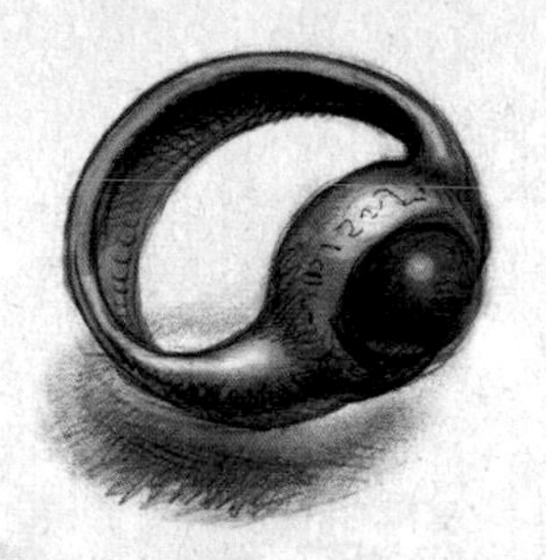

Traveler Ring

The most important possession of a Traveler, for it helps them find the gates to the flume. Through this ring, Bobby is able to send his journals to Mark and Courtney. Its stone is made from the same material as the flume.

Press Tilton

Traveler. Bobby's adventurous uncle.
He prepares Bobby to be a Traveler, then sends him off to meet his destiny.

THE LOST CITY OF FAAR

"This is the way it was meant to be."
—Uncle Press

The territory of Cloral

is a unique tropical habitat covered entirely by warm water. The people live on massive barges that hold everything from rich farmland to high-rise cities. They are as comfortable on these floating islands as they are underwater where farming, sports, and travel are commonplace. This is a society that has taken full advantage of nature to create an ideal world that is truly a tropical paradise and a glorious place to live.

Until people start mysteriously dying.

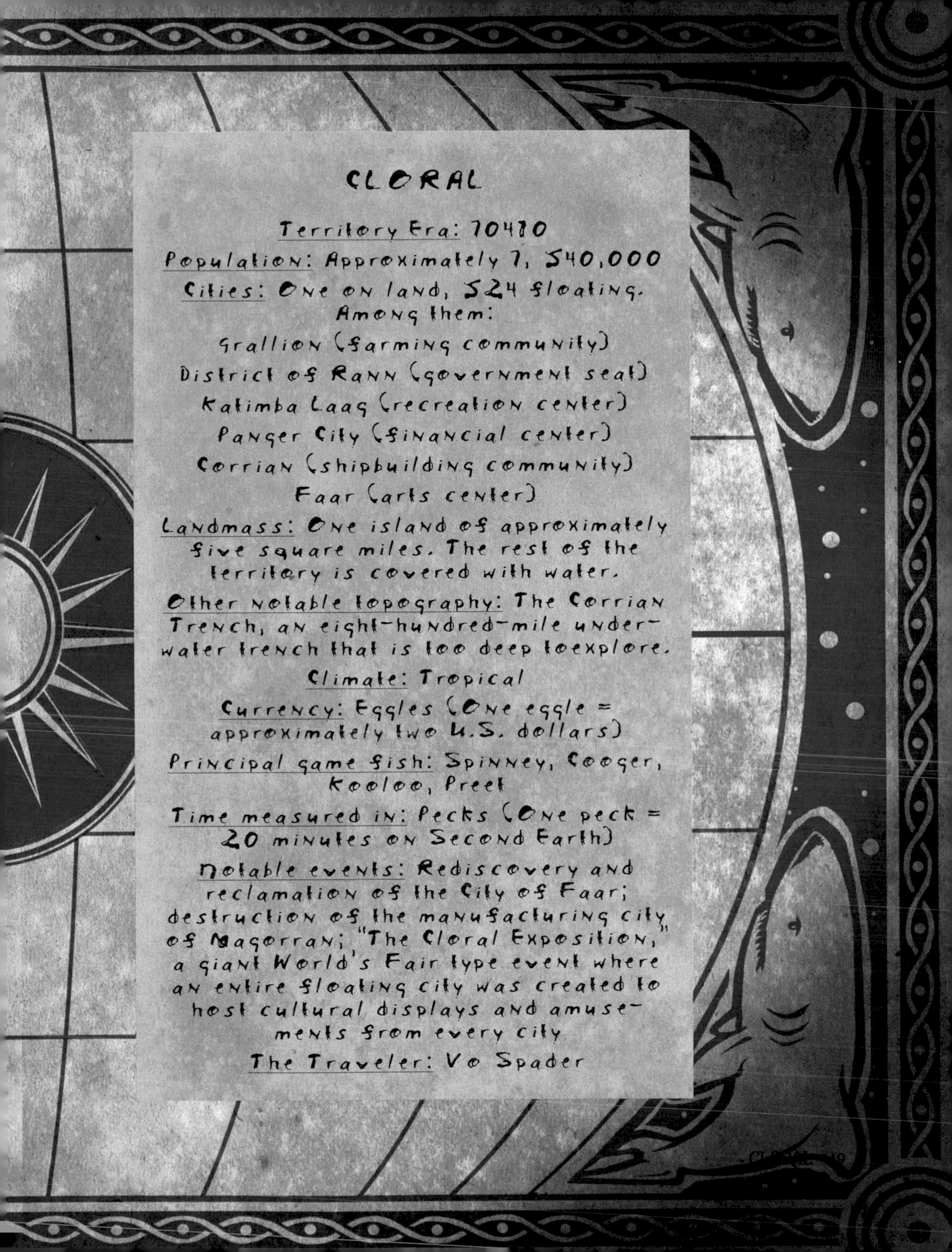

CLORAL

Territory Era: 70410

Population: Approximately 7, 540,000

Cities: One on land, 524 floating. Among them:

Grallion (farming community)

District of Rann (government seat)

Katimba Laag (recreation center)

Panger City (financial center)

Corrian (shipbuilding community)

Faar (arts center)

Landmass: One island of approximately five square miles. The rest of the territory is covered with water.

Other notable topography: The Corrian Trench, an eight-hundred-mile underwater trench that is too deep toexplore.

Climate: Tropical

Currency: Eggles (One eggle = approximately two U.S. dollars)

Principal game fish: Spinney, Cooger, Kooloo, Preet

Time measured in: Pecks (One peck = 20 minutes on Second Earth)

Notable events: Rediscovery and reclamation of the City of Faar; destruction of the manufacturing city of Magorran; "The Cloral Exposition," a giant World's Fair type event where an entire floating city was created to host cultural displays and amusements from every city

The Traveler: Vo Spader

An entire city is wiped out. The cause is a mysterious plague that attacks the food supply and could easily spread throughout the territory. Panic threatens to overcome paradise, aggravated by Saint Dane, who has taken the identity of a villainous pirate whose goal isn't to plunder treasure, but food.

Bobby and Uncle Press team with the Traveler from Cloral, an adventurous aquaneer named Vo Spader, to hunt down the source of this strange plague, and stop it before it kills again.

Skimmer

A one-man water vehicle that is used on the open ocean, as well as on the canals that snake through the floating cities of Cloral.

Water Sled

Used to propel swimmers under the waters of Cloral. It is a valuable tool while working the underwater farms.

Air Globe

This clear device morphs into a form-fitting, perfectly sealed helmet that allows swimmers to breath and communicate underwater.

Vo Spader

Traveler. An aquaneer who works on the floating farm of Grallion. He is a fun-loving guy who is always ready for adventure, but becomes consumed with hatred for Saint Dane after the demon kills his father.

They soon discover that the ultimate clue to saving Cloral may be hidden in a city that was thought to exist only in fable. A city that long ago sank beneath the ocean, never to be seen again. A city called Faar.

Spear gun

A quig-killer.

Spinney Fish

Normally thin and sleek, their bodies bloat to frighten off attackers. Spader likes to play Spinney-do by grabbing the ridges on their backs and riding them like bucking broncos.

THE NEVER WAR

"I'm scared about what we had to do to stop him."

—Bobby Pendragon, Journal #12

For Bobby, the battle against Saint Dane comes home. He has turned fifteen and learns that Earth actually holds three different territories. One is his own, the present. Another exists in the not-too-distant past. The third is centuries ahead in the year 5010. Saint Dane has targeted First Earth, the year 1937, to wage his next battle.

V-151 Schrek/Viking

The bone-chattering Coast Guard seaplane flown by Jinx Olsen.

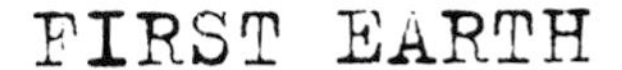

FIRST EARTH

<u>Territory era:</u> A.D. 1937

<u>Population:</u> approx 128,800,000 (Second Earth, in the year 2005, has approximately 6,400,000,000.)

<u>Landmass:</u> Seven continents making up

approximately 92.5 million square miles. Seventy percent of the territory is covered with water, making up approximately 224.5 million square miles.

<u>Movies:</u> A Day at the Races, starring the Marx Brothers; *Snow White & the Seven Dwarfs*

<u>Popular sport:</u> Baseball (New York Yankees defeat New York Giants for the professional championship)

<u>Radio broadcasts:</u> Notable performers include Edgar Bergen and Charlie McCarthy, Jack Benny, Bob Hope

<u>Notable books published:</u> *The Hobbit* by J.R.R. Tolkien; And to *Think That I Saw It On Mulberry Street,* the first book by Dr. Seuss

<u>Notable events:</u>

Destruction of the airship *Hindenburg* (event captured and broadcast as the first coast-to-coast radio broadcast)

Amelia Earhart, female aviator, disappears while attempting to fly around the world.

Opening of the Golden Gate Bridge

First cartoon starring Daffy Duck

<u>Time measured in:</u> minutes

<u>President of the United States:</u> Franklin D. Roosevelt

<u>Notable inventions:</u> ballpoint pen, photocopier, nylon, cellophane tape, first jet engine, electric digital calculator

<u>The Traveler:</u> Vincent “Gunny” VanDyke

Along with Vo Spader and the Traveler from First Earth, Gunny VanDyke, Bobby must tap his knowledge of history to unravel Saint Dane's next evil plot. The twisting trail brings them up against ruthless gangsters, enemy spies, pitiless murderers, a daring woman aviator, and a world on the verge of the bloodiest war in its history.

Maximillian Rose

A ruthless gangster who operates a spy ring out of the Manhattan Tower Hotel. Among his many criminal enterprises, he sells government secrets to the highest bidder, whether friend or foe.

Nancy "Jinx" Olsen

A pilot for the Coast Guard who longs for more adventure, and finds it.

Tommy Gun

The weapon of choice for Max Rose's band of hard-nosed gangsters.

Vincent "Gunny" VanDyke

Traveler. The bell captain of the Manhattan Tower Hotel. He's called "Gunny" because he cannot bring himself to fire a gun.

The grim reality is that the Travelers' battle for First Earth may be their most crucial yet, for a loss on First Earth could topple all three Earth territories. For Bobby, it would mean the destruction of his home and the loss of his best friends, Mark and Courtney. If this challenge isn't difficult enough, the Travelers find that they don't agree on how to win the fight. If they can't solve their own differences, they stand no chance of stopping Saint Dane from leveling Earth.

City Vehicle

Transportation Third Earth style in the Earth year of 5010.

LZ-129

The airship *Hindenburg*. It crashed and burned mysteriously on May 6, 1937, as it flew from its home in Germany to the U.S.

Winn Farrow

Nemesis of Max Rose who would stop at nothing to destroy Rose and his criminal empire.

The Empire State Building

Built in 1931, it is the tallest building on First Earth.

THE REALITY BUG

"You've made destroying Veelox such a pleasure!"

—Saint Dane

Imagine your wildest fantasy. No limits. No rules. No questions. Now imagine that it can all come true. This is what the territory of Veelox offers. An incredible virtual reality generator called Lifelight makes it possible. The people of Veelox spend their time in tiny cubicles, wired into Lifelight, living inside their own personal dreams of perfection. It's an illusion, but seems incredibly real. There's only one problem.

Reality.

Since the people of Veelox choose to live inside their own fantasies, their real world is crumbling. Literally. There is no one left to grow food, keep the lights on, repair the streets, or work to provide any of the basic needs of a modern society. The horrible truth is that by the time Bobby arrives, Veelox is already well on its way to destruction.

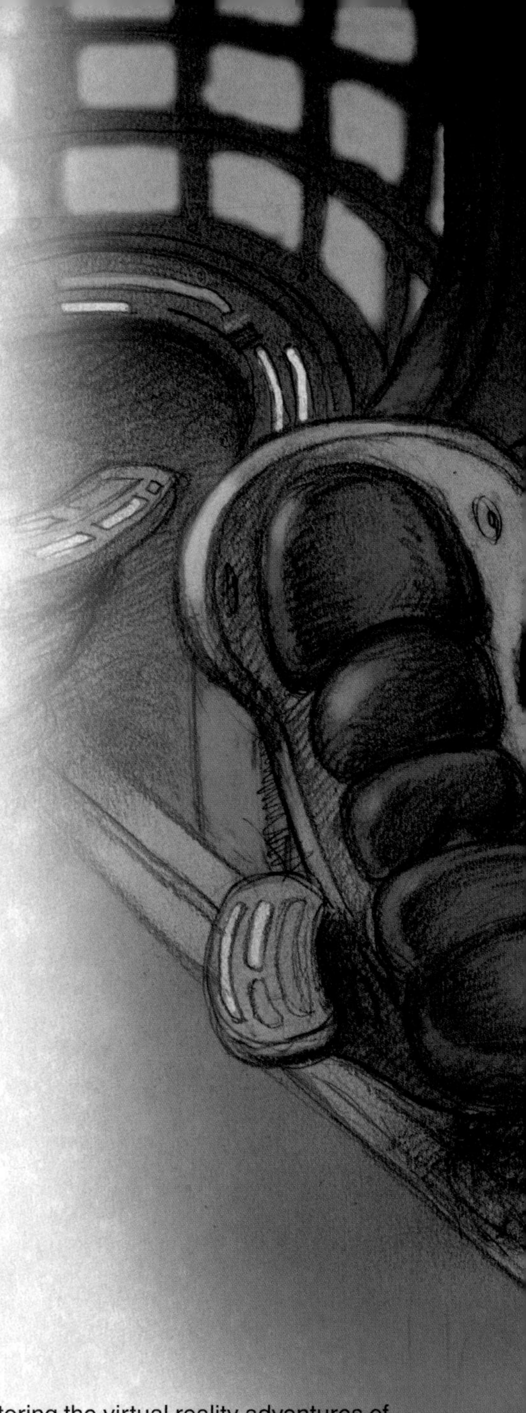

The Core

A phader busy at work, monitoring the virtual reality adventures of the jumpers inside the monster computer, Lifelight. Each jumper's personal fantasy can be seen as it unfolds on one of the millions of monitors that the phaders use to troubleshoot problems and keep the jumpers out of danger.

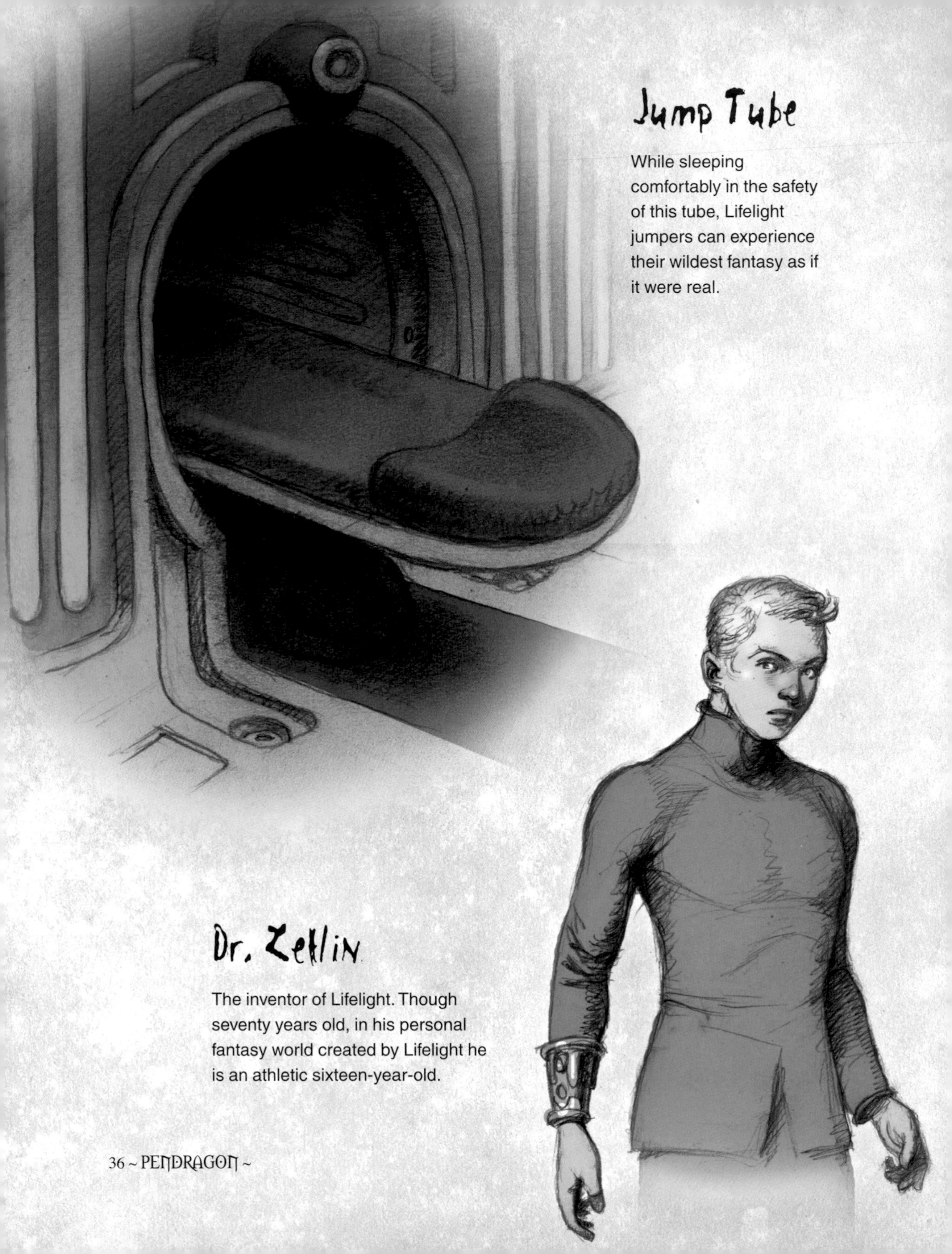

Jump Tube

While sleeping comfortably in the safety of this tube, Lifelight jumpers can experience their wildest fantasy as if it were real.

Dr. Zetlin

The inventor of Lifelight. Though seventy years old, in his personal fantasy world created by Lifelight he is an athletic sixteen-year-old.

VEELOX

Territory era: 45-226-9B
Population: 100, 000, 000
Population living inside Lifelight: Approaching 100, 000, 000
Number of Lifelight Pyramids in operation: Approximately 75,000
Landmass: Forty-seven continents. Twenty-four percent of the territory is covered by water.
Sociology: There are 212 sovereign countries, including: The Ibilik Federation (the largest and most powerful country)
Kanda (capital, Rubic City)
The Kingdom of See (smallest country, population of 651)
The Principal of Deelix (technology center where phaders and vedders are trained)
Currency: Rists (One rist = approximately 320 U.S. dollars)
Time measured in: Unets (One unet = approximately one minute)
Climate: Temperate throughout
Crops: Not applicable
Foods: Twelve varieties of gloid, a nutritional food supplement.
Recreation: No longer required
Notable events: None since the invention of Lifelight
The Traveler: Aja Killian

Saint Dane: Gunslinger

The fantasy image of Saint Dane that Bobby must battle on his Lifelight jump into the old West.

Saint Dane's plan was simple. He helped create Lifelight, knowing that the people would be seduced by it. It becomes the task of Bobby and the Traveler from Veelox, the brilliant Aja Killian, to find a way to scuttle Lifelight and restore sanity. To that end, they must leave reality and enter the fantasy world of a mad genius. But the dangers they find in this impossible realm, are all too real.

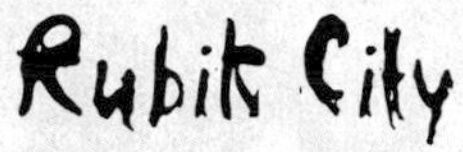

Rubik City

A Lifelight Pyramid towers over this once vibrant metropolis. The city has fallen into decay since most of the citizens have chosen to spend their time in the fantasy world of Lifelight, instead of reality.

Aja Killian

Traveler. Senior phader from Rubik City. The creator of the reality bug.

BLACK WATER

"And so we go."

—Bobby Pendragon, Journal #16

SAINT DANE HAS raised the stakes. He is no longer satisfied with attacking only the territories. In his mad quest to control Halla, he has chosen to eliminate the only force that stands in his way: the Travelers. Bobby must go to the jungle territory of Eelong to rescue the first Traveler who has been targeted: Gunny. Not knowing whether Gunny is dead or alive, Bobby arrives alone to discover a wild territory where danger lurks in every shadow.

Jungle Dweller

A monkey, Eelong style.

Kasha

Traveler. She is a forager, who must battle the ferocious tangs to collect food from the jungle floor to feed the klees.

Eelong is a tropical jungle with massive trees and a band of light in the sky made from many small suns. It may be beautiful, but Eelong is fraught with predators. Human-size lizards called tangs prowl the jungle floor, forcing the inhabitants of Eelong to live in the trees. They have built elaborate, multi-level cities high above the jungle floor to stay clear of the marauding tangs. These cities would seem to be a safe haven for Bobby. But the inhabitants pose a unique problem. They aren't human. Worse, Eelong is suffering from a devastating famine, and the inhabitants are about to pass a revolutionary law that may be the only way to save their race: They are going to make it legal to hunt and eat humans.

BLACK WATER
Leeandra Region
CLEFT
Continent of Ruum, including the distant Meeken Range of mountains.
LAKE
LEEANDRA
FIELDS

EELONG

<u>Territory era:</u> Unknown

<u>Landmass:</u> Five continents: Ruum, Oron, Tantan, Sheeg, and Habutta

<u>Notable geography:</u> Lake Ujenjo (freshwater lake fed by 53 waterfalls on the continent of Habutta), The Meeken Range (vast mountain range on the continent of Ruum where the colony of Black Water was established)

<u>Population:</u> Approximately 22,000,000 Klee & 46,000,000 Gar

<u>Climate:</u> Tropical

<u>Currency:</u> Kekks (One kekk = approximately 1.5 U.S. dollars)

<u>Energy:</u> Solar power gathered from the belt of small suns known as the Skaa that provide the territory's light and warmth.

<u>Time measured in:</u> Not applicable. Time is not measured.

<u>Major cities:</u> Leeandra (continent of Ruum); Benzara (continent of Sheeg); Saravara (continent of Oron); Black Water (continent of Ruum, newly discovered)

<u>Recreation:</u> Wippen (team sport played on zenzen horses), Kagel (individual sport of target shooting using small, metal disks)

<u>Notable events:</u> Revelation of the Gar colony of Black Water

First radio broadcast

Wippen Championship won by the North End Strikers of Leeandra.

<u>The Traveler:</u> Kasha

The vicious, meat-eating monsters of Eelong. They travel in packs and feed on any living creature they can sink their talons into.

Saint Dane

On Eelong he has taken the form of Timber, a member of the governing Council of Klee. He is working to repeal Edict Forty-six, which will allow klees (cats) to hunt and kill gars (humans).

The Traveler from Eelong, Kasha, isn't human and wants nothing to do with Bobby. Finding other allies is next to impossible, because on Eelong, humans are treated worse than animals. Bobby's single biggest challenge is to stay alive long enough to find Gunny. Without his trusted ally, he stands no chance of solving the mystery of the devastating famine and saving the territory from Saint Dane.

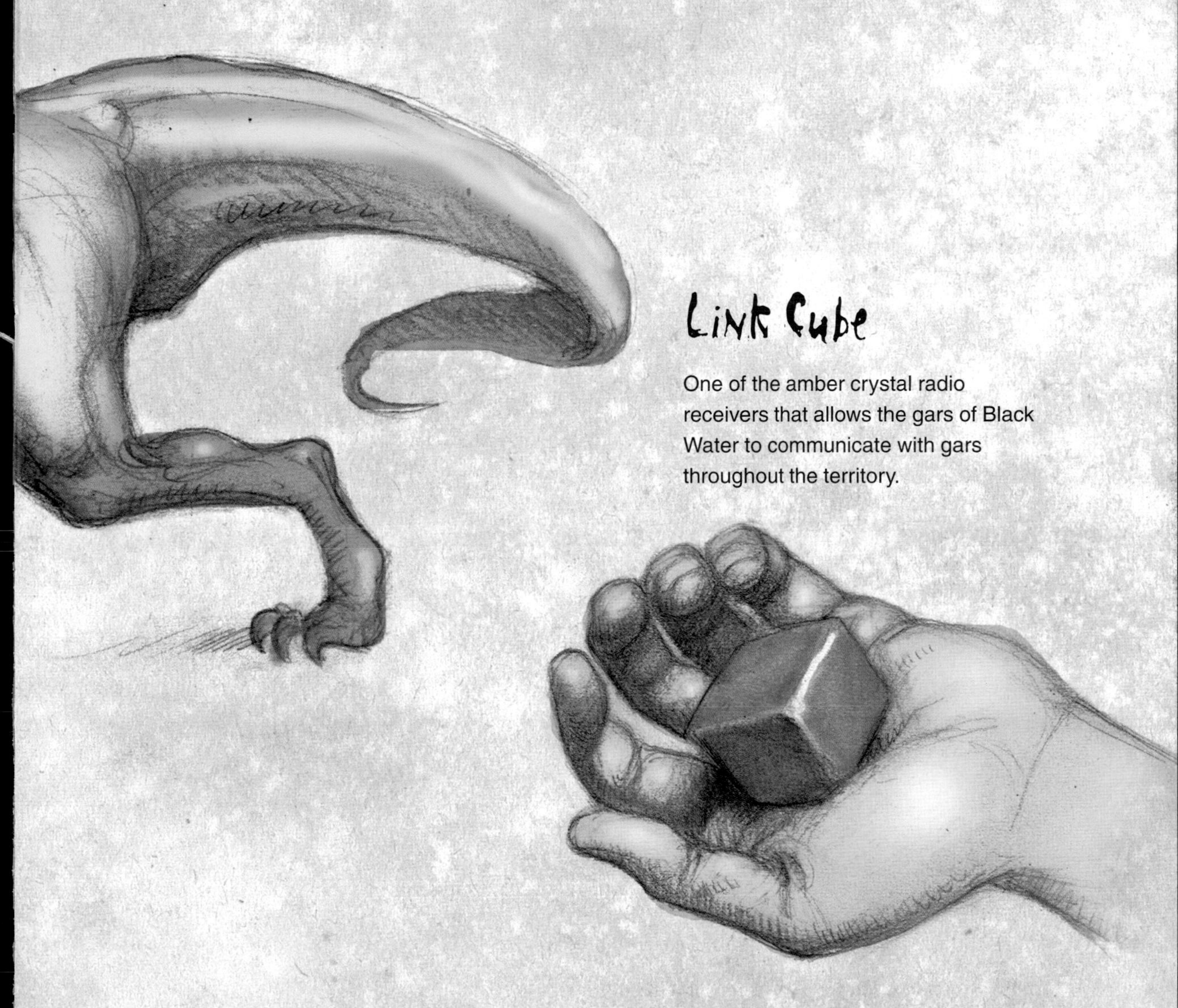

Link Cube

One of the amber crystal radio receivers that allows the gars of Black Water to communicate with gars throughout the territory.

BATTLES HAVE BEEN WON AND LOST. EVEN THOUGH Bobby Pendragon and his fellow Travelers have managed to keep Saint Dane from his ultimate goal of controlling Halla, the demon has been wearing them down. The grim truth is that even with the losses he's suffered, Saint Dane has been growing stronger. His assault on the territories will continue on to Zadaa, Quillan, Ibara, Third Earth, and horribly, Bobby's home—Second Earth. All are vulnerable to Saint Dane's evil. All are locked into his sights.

For Bobby, the ultimate mysteries remain: Why was he chosen to lead the Travelers? Where did Saint Dane come from and what is the source of his power? Most important of all, can Bobby stop Saint Dane and return to the life he misses so much?

Many truths will be revealed to Bobby, not only about Halla and the nature of existence, but about himself. With each new challenge, with every mystery unraveled, with every battle fought, the ominous truth grows all too clear: Before the fight for Halla can truly be won, there must be a supreme showdown between the two most powerful forces at the heart of the conflict. Only one can win. Only one will survive. At stake is the past, present, and future of all there is.

Because that's the way it was meant to be.